Herbie Jones
and Hamburger Head

Suzy Kline

illustrated by Richard Williams

Puffin Books

Acknowledgments
Special thanks to my editor,
Anne O'Connell, for her thoughtful,
hard work; for my husband, who brought
Hamburger Head home; and Mom,
who loves her cat, Martha.

PUFFIN BOOKS
Published by the Penguin Group
Viking Penguin, a division of Penguin Books USA Inc.,
375 Hudson Street, New York, New York 10014, U.S.A.
Penguin Books Ltd, 27 Wrights Lane, London W8 5TZ, England
Penguin Books Australia Ltd, Ringwood, Victoria, Australia
Penguin Books Canada Ltd, 10 Alcorn Avenue, Toronto, Ontario, Canada M4V 3B2
Penguin Books (N.Z.) Ltd, 182–190 Wairau Road, Auckland 10, New Zealand

Penguin Books Ltd, Registered Offices: Harmondsworth, Middlesex, England

First published in the United States of America
by The Putnam and Grosset Book Group, 1989
Published in Puffin Books, 1991
10
Text copyright © Suzy Kline, 1989
Illustrations copyright © Richard Williams, 1989
All rights reserved
Library of Congress Catalog Card Number: 91-53033
ISBN 0-14-034583-3

Lyrics from "How Much Is That Doggie in the Window" by Bob Merrill © 1952
® 1980 Golden Bell Songs. Used by permission. All rights reserved.
Lyrics from "Houndog" by Jerry Leiber and Mike Stoller, © 1956
GLADYS MUSIC AND MCA MUSIC (renewed). All rights administered by CHAPPEL & CO.
Used by permission. All rights reserved.

Printed in the United States of America
Set in Caledonia

*For Terry
and her parents, Bill and Virginia Chaplin,
with loving memories of our summer trips
and days of growing up*

Contents

1

Dr. Shadow

Herbie Jones sat on his front porch with his pal, Raymond Martin. Ray was looking for fleas on his dog, Shadow.

"Got one!" Ray said as he squished it between his fingers.

"You're lucky, Ray."

"Yeah, this bugger's dead."

"No, I mean, *you* have a dog," Herbie said, petting Shadow.

"Yeah, I like having a dog. They're helpful. If you forget your homework, you can always tell the teacher that your dog chewed it up."

"That worked *once* last year," Herbie grumbled.

"Hey, did you know my dog gives good financial advice?"

"Shadow gives financial advice?"

Ray nodded.

"Ray, you've been watching too much TV," Herbie said.

"You think so? Watch this. Are you ready, Dr. Shadow?"

"*Dr*. Shadow?" Herbie repeated.

"That's the code word. He knows I'm starting the advice trick. See?"

Herbie looked at Shadow. He was sitting up at attention and wagging his tail.

Ray put his ear next to the dog's mouth. "Uh, Shadow needs to know how much money you have in your baseball bank before he can give you advice."

Herbie rolled his eyeballs. "Five hundred sixty-eight pennies."

"Okay," Ray began. "Now, Dr. Shadow, please bark when I say what Herbie should spend his money on."

The dog looked up at Ray and didn't move.

"Should . . . Herbie keep all his money in his baseball bank?"

Shadow wagged his tail.

"Should . . . Herbie buy a new notebook for school?"

"I need one," Herbie said.

"Shhhh!" Ray scolded. "Dr. Shadow has to think."

Thump, thump, went Shadow's tail.

"Should . . . Herbie give his money to his sister Olivia?"

Thump, thump, went his tail again.

Herbie was relieved.

"Should . . . Herbie buy some cheeseburgers?"

"WOOF! WOOF!" Shadow barked.

Herbie stood up. "That doesn't count, Ray. You've been teaching him all summer to bark when someone says 'cheeseburger.'"

"WOOF! WOOF!" Shadow barked again.

"See?"

"Hey, it's good advice. Take it or leave it."

"What else can he do?"

"He growls when he spots thieves and murderers."

Suddenly, Shadow started growling in a low voice.

Herbie looked up. Annabelle Louisa Hodgekiss and Margie Sherman were walking down the street.

The boys cracked up.

"What's so funny?" Margie asked as they got closer.

"Nothing," they replied. The boys noticed the girls were walking their cats on leashes. Annabelle had a pink leash with rhinestones on it.

"Guess where we're going?" Margie asked, picking up her tiger cat.

"Where?" the boys replied.

"To the pet show down at the park. Aren't you going?"

Ray looked at Herbie. "Do you wanna?"

Herbie shook his head. "I don't have a pet, remember?"

"Well, if you're not going, I'm not going," Ray replied.

Annabelle's cat, Sukey, hissed at Shadow.

"It figures. You two are both deadheads. You don't do anything," Annabelle complained.

"We're gonna do *other* stuff," Herbie replied.

"So are we," Annabelle snapped as she pulled on the pink leash. "I'm getting my hair permed just as soon as I get back from the park. I want a new look for fourth grade."

"You could use one," Ray mumbled.

Annabelle flared her nostrils. "Raymond Martin, it's just as well you're not entering Shadow. They're not giving prizes for the most fleas."

As the girls stomped off, Annabelle turned around. "They're giving Burger Paradise coupons for prizes. Too bad you won't get one!"

Ray frowned. He didn't realize the winners got coupons.

Just then Mr. Jones stuck his head out the door. He was checking on the mail. "You boys being nice to the girls?"

"No problem, Dad."

After Mr. Jones flipped through the mail, he closed the squeaky door.

About a minute later, the boys heard the sound of the screen door again. Shadow was barking and Mr. Jones was bellowing.

"DON'T YOU KNOW THERE ARE NO

DOGS ALLOWED IN THIS HOUSE? OUT!"

Shadow came flying down the porch. When he reached Raymond, he nuzzled his nose in Ray's armpit.

"Don't take it personal," Herbie said, patting Shadow's back. "My dad acts that way to *all* dogs."

Shadow licked Herbie's hand.

"As a matter of fact, Dr. Shadow," Herbie said, "I think you give pretty good financial advice."

"The best!" Ray beamed.

"Summer is almost over," Herbie said. "I won't be needing much worm money. It's time to spend my life savings."

"On . . . ?" Ray was drooling.

"Cheeseburgers."

"WOOF! WOOF!" Shadow barked.

Ray jumped up in the air. "YAHOO!" he shouted.

The Pet Show

As the boys hurried down Washington Avenue, Herbie saw a big poster nailed to a telephone pole.

COME TO THE PET SHOW!
Thursday, Aug. 31st
Laurel Woods Park
2:00 p.m.–3:00 p.m.
PRIZES! FUN! COME!

Herbie looked at Ray. "Want to spy on them?"
"On who?"
"The kids at the pet show."
"I thought you didn't want to go."

"I don't. But spyin's different. Right, 992?"

Ray didn't feel like spying now. He wanted to bite into a cheeseburger.

"Come on, just a few minutes?"

"Okay," Ray grumbled.

The boys turned up Laurel Avenue and cut across the tennis courts. Shadow was trotting right behind them.

Herbie found a tall maple tree that overlooked the baseball diamond, where a group of boys and girls were gathering with their pets.

In the middle of the field was a table that had a banner that said "PET SHOW," and a tape player. The director of the park was standing behind the table holding a bunch of certificates and coupons and a megaphone.

Herbie set the baseball bank down on the lawn next to the tree trunk. "Shadow, you guard our money," he said.

Shadow lay down on the grass and put his chin on the bank.

Herbie and Ray climbed up the tree to the tallest branch. Herbie pushed some leaves aside so they could spy better.

"How come you're so interested in pets, when you can't have one?"

"Can't you like something you can't have?"

Raymond thought about it. "Yeah, you're right, Herbie. Most of the time I can't have a cheese-burger, and I *love* those things."

Herbie jabbed his buddy. "That's all you think about."

"Okay, Double 030, I hope this spying is good."

"Me too, 992," Herbie replied, leaning forward.

"BOYS AND GIRLS," the director called into the megaphone. "WE WILL BEGIN OUR PET SHOW! I WANT YOU TO WALK AROUND THE BASEBALL DIAMOND WITH YOUR PETS."

Herbie looked at the long line. Most of the kids had dogs or cats. He spotted two guys he knew from school. Phillip McDoogle had a boxer dog, and John Greenweed carried a bird in a cage. Herbie remembered John had an asthma problem. He was probably allergic to dog fur and cat hair. That's why his parents got him the bird, Herbie thought.

"I like that big brown mutt over there." Herbie pointed through the tree.

"I like this one," Ray replied, looking down at Shadow.

He was making dog snores under the tree.

"Yeah, Ray, he's a real Sleeping Beauty."

Just then the director put on a tape and everyone started to walk around the bases.

Annabelle was first in line with Sukey. She kept to the beat of the John Philip Sousa record by marching like a majorette. Herbie noticed how the rhinestones on her pink leash sparkled in the sun.

When she got to first base, Annabelle cut the corner square and held her head high. Herbie watched her braids swing around as she snapped her feet together at the corner.

Just as she paused a moment to take her harmonica out of her handbag (the one with her initials ALH on it), Sukey stood up on his hind legs and started batting at a bug with his left paw.

"Do you see that, Ray?" Herbie asked, making binoculars out of his fists.

"Sure do," Ray replied. "That cat could play for the Yankees. He just caught a fly at first base."

Herbie cheered. "What a southpaw."

Annabelle didn't notice.

But Herbie and Ray sure did. They were still laughing as the trail of pets rounded second and Annabelle played the song proudly on her harmonica.

Finally Herbie and Ray stopped laughing and caught their breath.

"Wanna go, Herbie? I'm tired of watching the Annabelle Show."

"Yeah, me too," Herbie agreed.

"But that Sukey Show wasn't bad," Ray added.

The boys laughed as they scooted down the tree.

3

Burger Paradise

Herbie and Ray dropped Shadow off at Ray's house and then hurried on downtown.

As soon as they got inside Burger Paradise, Ray pointed to a giant mobile hanging from the ceiling. "Just look at that!"

It was a huge hamburger with a tomato, pickle, lettuce, and Paradise Sauce. On either side of the buns were wings.

"Wow!" Ray exclaimed. "Isn't that the most beautiful thing you've ever seen in your life?"

Herbie held on to his baseball bank and stared at the crowd.

"It's a great-looking cheeseburger, Ray, but I'd like a seat while I'm eating one. This place is packed. Everyone must be doing back-to-school shopping."

"No problem. You stand in line and I'll find us a table."

Herbie studied the big menu. He turned around when he heard two girls behind him clapping hands. They were saying a chant as they clapped:

> "Girls go to college
> to get more knowledge.
> Boys go to Jupiter
> to get more stupider."

Herbie shot them a look, then turned around.

"Welcome to Paradise!" said a young man in a white cap. "May I take your order?"

Herbie knew exactly what he and Ray wanted. "Two cheeseburgers, two fries, and two sodas."

The young man in the white cap rang up the sale on the cash register. "That'll be four fifty-seven, please."

Herbie set his baseball bank on the counter. Then he unplugged the stopper and started counting.

After he made one pile of ten pennies, the young man raised his eyebrows. "*What* are you doing?"

"Counting out four hundred fifty-seven pennies."

The young man fiddled with his bow tie. "Excuse me a moment."

Herbie stacked another pile of ten pennies as the young man left. When he returned, he was standing next to an older man who had a name tag on. Herbie looked up and read it.

It said "Manager of Paradise."

The manager looked at Herbie's five piles of pennies.

"Fifty cents so far," Herbie beamed.

"Son, I'm sorry, but we can't take all these pennies."

"You can't?"

"It's too crowded to count them. Why don't you take your piggy bank . . ."

The two girls behind Herbie giggled.

22

Herbie was getting mad. "It is *not* a piggy bank, it's a *baseball* bank."

"Yes . . . well, take it to the Laurel Woods State Bank down the street. They have a new change machine. It wouldn't take long."

"I'll do that," Herbie said with an edge to his voice. Herbie picked up his piles of pennies, dropped them inside the bank, and put in the stopper.

Then he turned to the girls who had been bugging him with their giggles and stupid chants. "I have a verse for you."

They looked surprised. "You do?"

"It goes along with your Jupiter chant," and Herbie began:

> "Put the girls on Mars
>   behind iron bars,
>   while the boys explore
>   the moon and the stars!"

The two girls put their hands on their hips. Herbie smiled. The power of his poetry really got to them.

Now, if he could only get to Raymond.

Where was he?

Herbie looked around the crowded restaurant. Finally he spotted him at the only empty table. It was a long one by the window. Ray was sitting at the far end slurping on someone's leftover milk-shake. Herbie didn't notice the sign.

It said "Reserved."

"Ray!" Herbie scolded. "You don't know whose mouth has been on that drink!"

Ray had his eyes closed. "Mmmm, yes I do. Mine!" Then he burped.

Herbie shook his head. He pushed aside the empty paper cups and sat down.

"Put that cheeseburger right here," Ray said, tapping his side of the table.

"I have some bad news, Ray," Herbie said.

Raymond raised one eyebrow. "They ran out of Paradise Sauce?"

"Try again."

Just then a party of first-graders came into the restaurant. Each one was carrying a birthday gift.

Oh boy, Herbie thought. A bunch of babies right next to us.

"They ran out of pickles?" Ray asked.

"I have to go to the bank and get these pennies exchanged for bills. The manager said so."

Ray opened both eyes wide. "You mean we have to *wait* to eat until we go to the bank?"

Herbie nodded.

Ray looked at the party that had just joined them. Then he looked up at a girl in a white cap that said "Welcome to Paradise." She was passing out hats with halos on them.

"Don't forget us," Ray said with a silly grin.

Herbie shot Ray a look. "What are you doing?"

Ray put his halo on. "I like hats."

"I don't believe you," Herbie said, burying his head on the table. "You're going into fourth grade in one week."

When the girl returned, she carried a tray piled high with hamburgers and french fries. One by one she placed them in front of the boys and girls who were yelling and screaming at the birthday table.

When she got to Ray, she still had extras.

Suddenly, Ray got an idea. He adjusted his halo hat and then plopped one on Herbie. "We just love parties!"

The girl smiled back and placed a hamburger and fries in front of Ray and then Herbie.

Herbie adjusted his hat. The temptation was too much.

He looked around to see if he knew anybody. It was all clear.

Herbie peeled back the paper and bit into the juicy beef.

"Man, *this* is the life," Ray said, as some Paradise Sauce dripped from the corner of his mouth.

A few minutes later, the girl came back with sodas and coloring books for everybody.

The boys started slurping their sodas right away. They were thirsty.

When Herbie looked out the window, he thought he saw someone he knew.

It was John Greenweed and Phillip McDoogle coming down the street. They were carrying pet show certificates and coupons in their hands.

Herbie sank down in his chair. He hoped they didn't see him in his silly hat.

Then he heard a banging on the window.

Slowly Herbie looked up.

Phillip and John were laughing and pointing.

Ray waved.

"Come on, Ray, let's get outta here!"

Ray popped the last two fries in his mouth, then he eyed the extra hamburger on the tray. He grabbed it. He also tucked their coloring books under his arm.

Then he headed out the back door with Herbie.

John Greenweed and Phillip McDoogle were waiting for them.

"Well, look at the little angels. Aren't they cute?" Phillip McDoogle sneered.

Herbie gritted his teeth. Of all people, they had to be the ones to see them with the first-graders. No doubt John and Phillip were going to be in their fourth-grade class.

And he would be hearing about this *all* year.

Herbie pushed the boys out of his way and then stomped down the sidewalk.

Ray took off his hat and threw it at the boys as he followed Herbie down the street.

4

The Bank Robbery

Herbie looked up at the town clock. It was chiming three.

Bong! Bong! Bong! it sounded.

"Well, we don't have to go to the bank anymore. It's closed. Besides, we've already eaten."

Ray unwrapped his second hamburger. "Herbie, it's Thursday. The banks are open until six. I thought you needed a new notebook. They probably don't take pennies at Mr. D's either."

Herbie looked at his buddy. "What's in this for you? A *third* hamburger?"

Ray talked with his mouth full. "I was thinkin'

. . . I could use some new crayons to go with these coloring books."

Herbie looked at the books. He was glad Ray had another interest besides eating. Drawing. "Yeah, okay, let's get these pennies changed."

As the boys strolled down Main Street, they noticed an old run-down car parked in front of the Laurel Woods State Bank.

"Gee, Ray. Look at that license plate—it says 'Wyoming.'"

Ray stopped eating. "Wow! It's a rootin', tootin', shootin' cowboy's car. Do you s'pose he's in the bank?"

"Could be," Herbie said, walking over to the car. When he saw his reflection in the window, he shouted, "I STILL HAVE THIS DUMB HALO HAT ON! WHY DIDN'T YOU TELL ME, RAY?"

"I kind of liked it," Ray teased. "I've never hung around with an angel before."

Herbie socked his buddy in the shoulder. "You owe me one." Then he took the hat and threw it into the gutter.

As Herbie looked back at the car window, he

noticed a dog was waking up inside. "Look at that, Ray! There's a dog in the front seat."

Ray looked in. "Eewyee. He's gross! Look at his head."

Herbie watched the dog scratch his head with his paw. Blood rolled down the sides of his face. The skin was all ripped. There was a patch of flesh exposed on top of his head.

"Poor dog!" Herbie exclaimed. Then he looked at all the windows. They were rolled up tight. "Do you think he can breathe in there?"

Ray looked at their T-shirts. They were wet and sticky. "It's hot outside. Must be *real* hot in there. The windows should be open a little. That dog might suffocate."

Herbie tried the door handle. It wasn't locked.

Ray started to take another bite of his hamburger as he watched Herbie slowly open the car door and reach around for the window knob.

Suddenly the dog jumped out of the car.

"No, boy!" Herbie called. "Back inside. Ray, quick, hand me your burger."

"No way! There's at least two bites left!"

"You owe me one, remember?"

Reluctantly, Ray gave his half-chewed hamburger to Herbie. Herbie kneeled by the car seat and held it out to the dog. "Here, boy," he called again.

The dog walked over to Herbie, sniffed his hand and then the meat.

Herbie studied the dog closely. It looked like a raw hamburger patty was sitting on the dog's head.

He watched the dog gulp down the burger and lick his chops.

Then the dog turned, walked over to the curb, and picked up the halo hat in his teeth. When he brought it back to Herbie, Herbie laughed.

So did Ray. He was standing on the rubber mat that opened the bank door.

"Good dog," Herbie said, tossing the hat in the trash can. "Now, up you go on the seat."

"HURRY UP!" Ray shouted from the rubber mat.

The dog looked back at Raymond and then through the open door. Suddenly he spotted someone inside the bank and ran through the door.

"WAIT!" Herbie called, slamming the car door.

Quickly he darted into the bank after the dog.

The dog went right up to a tall blond lady in a raincoat and sniffed her shoe.

"It must be her dog," Ray said in a low voice.

"It's not raining," Herbie whispered to Ray as they stood in line behind the blond lady.

Ray looked down at the lady's feet. "She's wearing shoes that look like my dad's," he whispered back.

"What's she got in her pocket?" Herbie asked. She was pointing it at the teller.

The boys stood fixed, watching the dog jump up at the lady.

"Do you think she's a . . . a . . ." Herbie began to stammer.

Suddenly, the dog knocked something out of the lady's hand.

It bounced on the floor.

The boys looked.

It was a water pistol.

"IT'S A BANK ROBBERY!" the bank teller yelled as she ducked behind the counter.

Two bank officers with red polka-dot ties ducked under their desks.

Ray ran over to a potted palm tree and squatted behind it.

Herbie threw his baseball bank up in the air. It went flying into a marble bust of George Washington. The stopper popped out and so did the pennies.

All 568 of them!

Herbie quickly ducked behind the potted palm tree next to Ray.

The lady bolted for the door with the dog. When they got halfway, she and the dog slipped on the pennies and slid across the floor.

The lady's blond wig came off, and the stack of bills she had stashed in her pocket flew to either side.

Ray's eyes bulged. He had never seen thousand-dollar bills before.

Three police cars with sirens screeched to a stop in front of the bank. Six police officers stormed inside.

When they looked around, they saw the robber on the floor and the dog holding a blond wig in his mouth.

The police chief spoke first. "Handcuff him,

men, and get the wig. That's Joe Barona from Wyoming! He's wanted for robbery in four states."

The dog barked when they dragged Joe Barona to the police car.

"It's okay, everyone," the police chief said. "You can come out now!"

Herbie stepped out. The dog walked over to him and licked his hand.

A news reporter came running into the bank with a camera. "What happened?" he asked as he took a pencil off his ear.

The bank officers stood up from behind their desks. The bank teller peeked over the counter.

"That dog came into the bank and knocked the water pistol out of the robber's hand. As soon as I knew it wasn't a loaded gun, I yelled, 'ROBBERY,'" the teller said.

The reporter wrote words on his pad.

"That boy over there dropped his piggy bank—"

"Baseball bank," Herbie corrected.

"—and his pennies spilled all over the floor," the teller continued. "That's what tripped up the robber."

"So . . . " the reporter said as he kept on writ-

ing, "this dog and this boy are heroes?"

Everyone nodded.

Ray was still hiding behind the potted palm tree. Finally, he stepped out. "Would you like some help picking up the thousand-dollar bills?"

The bank officers smiled. "You can help pick up the pennies, son. How many did your friend have?"

"Five hundred sixty-eight," Herbie chimed in. "I wanted to get it changed for bills."

"I'll take care of that for you," the bank teller said.

The reporter put the pencil back on his ear. "Okay, kid, you come over here and stand next to this bust of George Washington with your dog."

My dog, Herbie thought. "Just a minute, sir, I have to talk to my friend." Herbie walked over to Ray, who was picking up the 568 pennies.

"Ray," Herbie whispered, "what do you think is gonna happen to that dog?"

"Well, when they find out he belongs to the robber, they'll take him to the pound. If no one wants him, he'll be put to sleep in four days."

Herbie stared at the dog's head. It looked gross. Who would want him for a pet?

"Huh?" the reporter said when Herbie returned. "What's your dog's name? He sure got wounded in battle. The robber must have fallen on his head."

"Uh . . . his name?"

"Yeah, and yours. I need your address, too, for the story."

Herbie gave his first. "Herbie Jones, one-oh-five Washington Avenue."

"And your dog?"

Herbie got down on his knees and cupped his hands around the dog's face. His brown eyes looked sad. The top of his head did look like ground hamburger.

The reporter was getting an edge to his voice. "I have a deadline to meet, kid. What's the name of your dog?"

"Hamburger Head," Herbie said.

"Unusual name," the reporter said, writing it down. "Okay, hold your dog next to this George Washington statue. And smile."

Herbie slowly picked up the dog. It was like lifting a ten-pound sack of flour. The dog licked Herbie's ear. It tickled so much that Herbie laughed.

Click, went the camera.

"You'll be in tomorrow afternoon's paper, kid!" the reporter said, dashing out of the bank.

After the bank officer gave Herbie five crisp one-dollar bills and some change, Herbie picked up his baseball bank and walked out with Ray.

The dog followed them.

"Well," Ray said as he stepped on the rubber mat, "you're a big shot now. I can't wait for John Greenweed and Phillip McDoogle to see your picture in the paper."

Herbie stopped at the trash basket in front of the bank. The dog had knocked it over and was nosing his way through the paper, banana peels, coffee cups, and candy wrappers.

When he found what he was looking for, he grabbed it with his teeth and walked it over to Herbie. He was wagging his tail.

It was the hat with the halo.

Herbie sank to his knees and patted the dog's back. "What am I going to do with you, Hamburger Head?"

Ray squatted down next to them. "You're gonna have to be his angel, Herbie, and find him a home."

5

Big Plans
at Annabelle's House

After the boys stopped at Mr. D's and picked up a red notebook and a package of eight crayons, they headed down Fish Street.

"Maybe somebody in the neighborhood could take him," Herbie said. "How about *you*, Ray? I could visit him a lot if you took him."

Ray shook his head. "I have a dog, remember? Mom would never let me have two. Besides, Shadow might get jealous and have a heart attack. He's getting old, you know."

The boys looked up the street. There was Annabelle's house. They saw the girls coloring on Annabelle's front porch. Annabelle's hair was up in tiny pink curlers.

Herbie thought she looked like his mother.

He decided to be friendly. Maybe they could help find a home for the dog.

"Hi, girls," he called in a cheerful voice.

The girls looked up. Margie waved. Annabelle grabbed Sukey as soon as she saw the dog. "Is he friendly?"

"Very," Herbie replied.

Sukey ran in the house through the little pet door.

Annabelle walked over to the dog. "What happened to his head? It looks like he tore his skin off!"

"He did."

Annabelle took a step back. "Just a minute, I have to get something."

When she returned, she had her doctor's kit. She took out a surgical mask and surgical gloves. After she put them both on, she moved closer to examine the dog.

"You should keep your face covered all the time," Ray said. "It's a great improvement."

Herbie jabbed his buddy. Annabelle was being helpful. He didn't want to get her angry. He was glad she was concentrating so hard she didn't hear Raymond.

Margie joined them. "Eewyee, the poor dog. What happened?"

Annabelle took out a magnifying glass and bent over. "He scratched the skin right off his head," Annabelle said like a scientist. "It's probably just a bad case of fleas, but he should see a vet right away. You could take him to my vet, Dr. Nguyen. She's very good. The only thing is, it would cost around twenty-five dollars. Whose dog is it?"

"It's—" Herbie was interrupted by Ray, who blurted out about the bank robbery, how Herbie was a hero, and how the dog belonged to the robber, Joe Barona.

Annabelle took off her surgical mask and gloves. "Herbie, is he telling one of his big, big stories?"

"Nope. Every bit is true."

Annabelle dropped her mask and gloves on the lawn. She didn't say anything for a long minute.

"Well," she finally continued, "no one will want a dog in this condition. Except maybe you, Herbie. Why don't you keep him?"

Herbie frowned. "My dad says dogs are a nuisance, they cost money and they smell up the place."

"He won't even let 'em go in their house," Ray added.

"Could you keep him in your backyard for a few days?" Annabelle suggested. She started to pet him and then remembered his bloody head.

Herbie shrugged. "Maybe . . ."

"What's his name?" Margie asked.

"Herbie told the reporter it was Hamburger Head," Ray replied.

Annabelle tried not to laugh. She felt sorry for the dog. "We have to get him to the vet."

Herbie reached in his pockets. "Will three dollars and some change help?"

Margie waved her hands in the air. "My parents had a tag sale last weekend. We could earn money if *we* had one."

Ray looked at his T-shirt. He had it on backward. "I gotta tag right here. It says 'large' and 'a hundred percent cotton' on it." He ripped it off and handed it to the girls. "How much could we get for this one?"

Annabelle groaned. "Raymond, a tag sale is like

a garage sale."

"Oh," Ray replied. "Well, I can't help. I could never sell *our* garage."

"You sell *used* stuff at a tag sale, Ray," Herbie said. "And if we had one bright and early tomorrow morning at my house, we could earn money for Hamburger Head's vet fee. Could you guys bring stuff to sell?"

"We're not guys, Herbie," Annabelle corrected. "But we could. It's for a good cause, right, Margie?"

Margie beamed. "I've got lots of things I could sell."

Herbie clicked his fingers. "We could call it a 'wag sale' because all the profits go for a dog!"

Everyone smiled.

"Why don't we make signs for the wag sale right now?" Ray suggested. He had been thinking about drawing ever since Herbie bought him the new crayons at Mr. D's.

Annabelle ran into the house. "I'll get some big paper."

When she returned, she picked up her big box of sixty-four crayons off the porch. "We may have a problem," she said.

"What's that?" Herbie asked.

"Ray can't use my crayons anymore. He colors too hard."

Ray made a toothy smile. "No problem."

The girls watched him reach into his jeans pocket like a cowboy going for his gun and pull out his pack of crayons. "I'm ready to draw!"

Annabelle raised her eyebrows. She had never seen Ray take anything out of his pockets but burned-out fuses.

"Good," Annabelle replied. "Now, Herbie, I'll show you which crayons *you* may use."

Herbie shook his head. "Never mind, I'll use Ray's."

Annabelle looked relieved. "Now, everyone remember to spell 'wag sale' correctly," Annabelle continued.

"A piece of cake," Ray said as he took a nice pointy purple crayon out of his box.

As they all worked on their posters, Hamburger Head moved next to Herbie. He put his black nose close to Herbie's green crayon. When it fell out of his hand and rolled down the steps, Hamburger Head ran after it.

Annabelle put down her periwinkle crayon. She

noticed the dog returned the green crayon to Herbie and then nuzzled close to his side.

"He likes you," Annabelle said.

Herbie looked at the dog. That's what made it hard to finish his poster. He was beginning to like the dog too.

Herbie decided to make some words smaller.

6

Hamburger Head
Meets Mr. Jones

Hamburger Head carried the halo hat in his teeth as he followed the boys down Wainwright Crescent. Herbie carried the posters.

When they came to Ray's house, Ray ran up his porch steps. "I'll get some Chunky Chow Bits for you to take home. Shadow has lots."

Just then Shadow came across the tall lawn. All Herbie could see was his black nose above the grass. The Martins didn't mow their lawn much, Herbie thought.

When Shadow got to the sidewalk, he sniffed Hamburger Head's neck. Then he growled in a low voice.

Herbie knew what that meant.

Shadow thought Hamburger Head was a thief or a murderer.

Suddenly Shadow grabbed the halo hat from Hamburger Head. Hamburger Head pulled in the other direction.

The halo hat split in two. Each dog had a piece in his mouth. And each was growling at the other.

Herbie pulled Hamburger Head away. Shadow trotted back to the porch and chewed on his treasure. Ray came outside and stepped over him.

"I can tell they're gonna be great friends," Ray said. "They're sharing things already."

Herbie half smiled. He was glad to be rid of the halo hat, anyway.

"Sorry, pal," Ray said, coming down from the porch. "We're all out of Chunky Chow Bits. Mom left a note on the table saying she went to the store. I'll get some to you this weekend."

"Thanks, Ray. I gotta get him out of here. See you tomorrow. Bring lots of good stuff at eight-thirty sharp."

"Right on. I'll bring some real neat things!"

Herbie looked at his buddy. He wondered about those neat things.

As Herbie walked along the side of his house, Hamburger Head stopped to smell the gardenia bush next to the garbage can.

When Herbie opened the back screen door, he whispered to the dog, "You stay here on the welcome mat. My dad doesn't allow dogs in the house."

Herbie walked inside.

His dad was talking to his mother. "Why can't I have this can of SpaghettiOs?"

"The doctor told us to watch our weight. We're middle-aged now, and we have to eat more fruit and vegetables."

"So it's green salad again?" Mr. Jones complained as he looked at the bowls on the table.

"Yes, but I'm adding something else."

"SpaghettiOs?"

Mrs. Jones made a face. "Bean sprouts and alfalfa!"

"BEAN SPROUTS AND . . . HERBIE!" Mr. Jones was surprised to see his son standing by the back door. "Where have you been?"

"At Annabelle's."

"You've had five phone calls! Two from the *Laurel Woods Bee*, one from the president of the Laurel Woods State Bank, and two from friends."

Mrs. Jones rushed over to her son. "Were you in a bank robbery today?"

Herbie nodded.

Mrs. Jones hugged her son. "The bank president, Mr. LoPreato, raved about you, Herbie. We're so proud and happy you're okay. And that dog! He saved everybody, didn't he?"

"Whose dog was it?" Olivia asked.

Herbie explained the whole story, and when he finished, he pointed to the screen door. "He's out there."

Mr. Jones, Mrs. Jones, and Olivia walked to the back porch. They looked at the dog through the screen door. And then at the welcome mat. He had retrieved everything from the backyard. It was on the porch step next to him.

Olivia started to laugh. "Look at the stuff, Dad, that was on our lawn! Your socks off the clothesline, an old newspaper, my running shoes, Mom's old paperback book, and our sprinkler."

"The sprinkler?" Mr. Jones replied. "I've been

looking for that for ages!"

"Let this famous dog in for a minute," Olivia said. "I want to see him in person."

Herbie opened the screen door. The dog didn't budge. "It's okay, come on in."

Hamburger Head walked in and sat in the middle of the kitchen floor.

"Gross!" Olivia groaned. "What's wrong with his head? Does he have a disease?" She took a step back.

"It's a flea problem. He probably got a bad case of it from the car the bank robber kept him in. Me and my friends are having a wag sale tomorrow to earn money to take him to the vet."

"My friends and I," Olivia corrected. "Who is going to take care of him?"

"I want to," Herbie said.

Mr. Jones pointed to the back door. "There are *no dogs* allowed in this house! Out he goes!"

"I was hoping he could stay in our backyard, Dad, just for the weekend. I'm gonna try to find a home for him." Herbie swallowed hard.

Mrs. Jones put her arm around her son. "Sounds like you're getting attached to this dog."

Mr. Jones made a face. "Don't get any big ideas. We're not taking on any pets. But if you want to let him stay in our backyard for a few days, I guess it's okay. That Mr. LoPreato wants to meet him tomorrow night. Can you clean him up, Herbie?"

Herbie started to jump up and down. "Yes, Dad. Thanks, Dad. I'll keep him out of your way, Dad!"

"What are you going to feed him?" Mrs. Jones asked.

"He eats stuff we eat."

Mrs. Jones held up the can of SpaghettiOs. "Do you think he'd like this? I'm trying to get rid of the starch in this house. We must have six cans of it in our cupboard."

Mr. Jones made a face.

Herbie took the can opener and poured some on a plate. "Let's see."

The Joneses bent down and watched the dog smell the food. Immediately, the dog started lapping it up.

"Obviously, the dog has good taste," Mr. Jones grumbled.

Olivia watched Hamburger Head lick the plate clean. There wasn't one drop of tomato sauce left, or one little O.

"Well, he sure makes my scraping job easy," Olivia said as she picked up the plate and added it to the pile of dirty dishes.

"I'll take him out and wash him up," Herbie said.

"We're going out to dinner tomorrow night with Mr. LoPreato," Mrs. Jones called to her son. "He wants Ray to come along too. Isn't that nice?"

Mr. Jones sat down at the table and stared at his alfalfa salad. "It sure will be. I can't wait to have a real meal."

That night Herbie laid out a blue blanket on the grass just under his bedroom window. As he leaned out to say good night, he said a prayer:

"Dear God, if you decide to do any miracles this weekend, I sure would like it if you could arrange to have my dad like Hamburger Head. Amen."

Hamburger Head put his head on his paws and closed his eyes.

"'Night,' Burger Head," Herbie called.

Then he took out his red notebook and wrote a poem:

> Hamburger Head
> goes to bed
> on a blue blanket below.
> I think he's neat,
> I hope he sleeps
> underneath the stars and Mars,
> where all the girls are behind
> iron bars.

Herbie smiled, then he turned out the light.

7

The Wag Sale

Friday morning when Herbie woke up, he found Hamburger Head lying on his chest just staring at him. His paws were on his pajama pockets.

"How did you get in here?" Herbie said, sitting up. Then he looked over at the bedroom window. He had forgotten to close it, it was such a warm night.

"You jumped in all by yourself!" Herbie said as he looked at the dog's head.

"Hey! The top of your head is turning brown. You're getting scabs! You're healing!"

Herbie leaped out of bed. "YAHOO!" he shouted.

Olivia stuck her head around Herbie's door. "People are trying to sleep, Erb!"

Herbie stood in front of the dog. He didn't want his sister to see him. "Sorry, Olive."

When she closed the door, Herbie quickly picked up the dog and lowered him over the windowsill into the garden. "Now you stay outside. If my dad sees you in the house, it's all over. Understand?"

Hamburger Head barked.

"Shhh! You'll wake up my dad. He sleeps until two. He works the night shift."

Herbie thought it was neat to talk with a dog. Hamburger Head wagged his tail and then ran around to the welcome mat on the back porch.

Herbie met him there after he got dressed. He let the dog finish his bowl of cereal, then they walked around to the front of the house to wait for Ray.

Herbie set up the posters first. He put his on the mailbox on the porch.

Hamburger Head plopped down under the "Free Dog to Good Home" sign.

Herbie took out the other posters. Annabelle's poster had the words "Wag Sale," colored in gold.

A small dog was lost in a garden of roses, daisies, petunias, and sweet peas. Herbie thought her poster would have been good for a flower sale. He put it next to the bush by the porch.

Herbie liked Margie's. Hers said "Help a Dog. Buy Something." She had a dog in a rainstorm. Margie made neat forked lightning, Herbie thought. He hung her poster on the telephone pole.

Raymond's poster was a Viking ship with two big sails on it. On board was a dog wearing a Viking helmet. Raymond had printed "Wag Sail" in purple above the ship.

Annabelle had drawn a black X through the word "Sail" and written "Sale" above it. She said there could be no misspelled words.

Herbie liked it better Ray's way. He put his poster on the tree in the middle of his front yard.

At eight-thirty, Raymond arrived. He was pulling a wagon with a big box.

"Put your stuff down wherever you like," Herbie said, pointing to the blankets on the lawn and the TV trays.

Ray did.

Then he looked at Herbie's things. "You're sell-ing your baseball bank? And your Monopoly and Clue games? But there's nothing missing from them."

Herbie looked at Hamburger Head. He had his chin on his paws and was watching the boys. "It's for a good cause," Herbie said. Then he walked over and looked at Ray's stuff. "Does this jack-in-the-box work?"

"No," Ray said. "It belonged to my granddad. I got it in the attic."

"Is the wagon from your attic too?" Herbie asked.

Ray nodded.

Herbie noticed it had only three wheels.

When he saw the Burger Paradise coloring books, he picked them up and flipped through them. Half the pages were colored.

Herbie wondered if they should call their wag sale a junk sale.

Just then Olivia showed up at the door in her bathrobe. She had a pile of clothes in her hand, some tapes and records. "Can you use these?"

"Yeah! Thanks, Olive."

"Well," she said, looking down at the dog, "he looks disgusting now, but maybe after he sees the vet he'll get better and I'll be able to pet him."

Herbie beamed. His sister always came through.

At nine A.M., the girls showed up. Margie had a big box in her arms. Annabelle wheeled in a lawn mower and a framed poster of daisies with a blue ribbon on it.

"Isn't Annabelle's hair pretty?" Margie said.

Annabelle fluffed her hair. "Well, what do you think of my curls?"

Herbie looked at Annabelle. Her hair fell to her shoulders like corkscrews. "Nice," he said. "They remind me of the twisty noodles Mom uses in her tuna casserole."

Annabelle put her hands on her hips.

"I love tuna casserole!" Herbie added.

Annabelle decided to let it go.

"Isn't Annabelle great to bring her prize-winning daisy poster for our wag sale?" Margie said.

Ray gritted his teeth. He remembered that poster. It won the third-grade poster contest by one vote. His came in second.

Annabelle beamed. "Original art is worth a lot of money. What do you think I should charge?"

"A nickel?" Ray tried to be helpful.

Herbie wasn't listening. He was looking at the lawn mower.

"Funny, Raymond. I think five dollars would be a bargain," Annabelle said as she began to price the items.

Ray raised his eyebrows, then walked over to the cash register on the card table. "Who brought this? How much is it?" When he hit the red button, the drawer popped out with a ring.

"Neato!" Ray exclaimed.

Annabelle stepped in front of him. "It's mine, and it's *not* for sale. We'll use it to keep the money for the wag sale in."

While Margie laid out dolls, puzzles, books, and comics on a blanket, Herbie pushed the lawn mower. "It works!" he said.

"Of course it does. Do you think I would sell something that doesn't?"

Herbie looked at Ray.

"Well," Annabelle continued, "I'll just label everything." And the boys watched her take out little colored pieces of paper and a Magic Marker from her purse.

When she spotted the jack-in-the-box and the wagon, she stopped. "We can't sell these. They're broken!"

She put the box and wagon behind the tree and after another ten minutes she said, "I think we're ready now."

Herbie looked up at the porch. Hamburger Head was licking his lips. What was he eating? Where did he get it?

Herbie rushed up the stairs to investigate. There, next to the dog, was an empty package marked "Bean sprouts." Herbie turned and looked through the front screen door. His dad was snoring away in his big green chair.

"So, that's how Dad figures on getting rid of this stuff," Herbie said to the dog. "Well, let's hope he finds you real useful!"

Hamburger Head just licked his chops.

During the next hour, people came. Mothers, children, and teenagers. Cars stopped when they saw the signs and people gathering.

One elderly woman bought Herbie's baseball bank.

Raymond stepped over to the cash register and started to hit the red button. Annabelle pushed him aside and said, "The person whose item is sold gets to push the red button. Herbie makes this sale."

Raymond folded his arms. He hated it when Annabelle got so bossy.

He watched Annabelle walk over to the elderly lady who had just bought the baseball bank and ask, "Would you care to buy a lovely, original, prize-winning poster?"

"Hmmm, where is it?" the lady asked.

Annabelle held up her painting.

"No, I don't think so," the lady replied.

Annabelle frowned.

Then the lady noticed the sign for the dog on the mailbox. "I am interested in the 'free dog to good home.' Where is he?"

Herbie began to get worried.

Annabelle pointed to the porch. The lady walked up the stairs. "I think he's a golden retriever. They are such gentle dogs."

Suddenly the lady stopped when she saw the top of the dog's head. "Oh, my goodness, I couldn't have *that* in my house," she said, and left the wag sale.

Herbie breathed a sigh of relief.

When a man bought the lawn mower, Annabelle danced over to the cash register and said, "I'm making a ten-dollar sale!"

Herbie thought her noodle curls were fun to watch when they bounced.

Ray glared as she hit the red button and the drawer popped out. He hadn't had a turn to ring it all morning.

At noon, Annabelle marked down her painting from $5 to $2.50. Three teenagers and one man asked about the free dog, but as soon as they found out it was Hamburger Head, they changed their minds.

Herbie was pleased.

At one-thirty P.M., a man in a fancy car pulled up.

"Here comes someone with taste," Annabelle said as she propped her painting up on a chair.

The man in the red-striped tie glanced at the painting and then stopped by the tree. "How much is this jack-in-the-box?"

Annabelle looked shocked. "That's broken. I didn't even tag it."

"Whose is it?"

Raymond stepped forward. "It belonged to my granddad."

"I *thought* it was old. Would you take fifteen dollars for it?"

Ray made a toothy smile. "Sure will."

Annabelle flared her nostrils.

Ray hit the red button. Then he added a "Ta dah . . ." just before the drawer popped out.

"We have enough for the vet now!" Ray said.

Annabelle lowered the price of her daisy painting. She crossed out the $2.50 and made it $1.00.

"We haven't sold everything yet," she said. And then she walked up and down the sidewalk, calling, "ORIGINAL PRIZE-WINNING ART FOR SALE."

Herbie whispered to Ray, "We have to do something about Annabelle. This is getting sad."

Ray shrugged.

Herbie walked over to the cash register and pulled out a dollar bill. "Hey, Annabelle," Herbie called.

Annabelle turned. "What is it, Herbie?"

"I want to buy your painting for a dollar."

"You do?" Annabelle brought it over and admired it. "You have good taste, Herbie Jones. Where do you plan to hang it?"

Herbie didn't expect her to ask him that. He tried to think fast. Olivia and his parents wouldn't want it in their bedrooms. Herbie knew he didn't want it in his. The living room was out. So was the kitchen. What room was left?

"Hmmm?" Annabelle asked.

"Uh . . . I think it would be perfect in our bathroom."

"Your *bathroom?*" Annabelle's face turned red.

"Well," Herbie explained, "in a bathroom you want everything fresh as a daisy. Your picture has lots of daisies."

Annabelle clapped her hands. "It does! A marvelous choice, Herbie!"

Herbie looked at Ray and rolled his eyeballs. He was glad to get out of that one.

And the wag sale was over!

8

The SpaghettiOs

Just as everyone was cleaning up the front lawn, the newspaper boy came riding by on his bike. "You made the headlines, Herbie!" he shouted.

Then he tossed the paper up on the porch. It hit the railing and fell back into the garden behind the bush.

Mr. Jones was standing at the screen door. "I wish he had a better aim," he grumbled.

Hamburger Head jumped off the porch, nosed his way through the bush, and pulled out the newspaper. He ran it back up the stairs and handed it to Mr. Jones.

"Well, I'm glad I don't have to twist my body into a pretzel to get tonight's paper. Thanks, Hamburger Head," said Mr. Jones. And he took the paper from the dog's mouth.

Herbie noticed that the dog followed his father into the house. "Come on, guys, let's go see," Herbie said.

Annabelle, Margie, and Ray followed Herbie into the living room. They stood behind the green chair and looked over Mr. Jones's shoulders.

"There you are, Herbie!" Mr. Jones said proudly. "Right on the front page of the *Bee*."

"Good shot of George Washington," Ray said.

"You have your T-shirt on?" Annabelle groaned. "I would think you would put on a tie or something."

"I didn't wear a tie to the bank, Annabelle," Herbie grumbled.

"Look how cute Hamburger Head looks," Margie said. "You can't tell his head is gross in the picture."

The dog sat down next to Mr. Jones's feet.

"Read the article, Mr. Jones," Ray said. "There are too many big words for me."

Annabelle flared her nostrils. "I'll be happy to read it," and she did so with expression:

Boy, Dog Foil Bank Robbery
By Fred Storey

LAUREL WOODS, August 31— A robbery attempt was foiled today when a brave dog and a resourceful boy saved the Laurel Woods State Bank $50,000.

The dog, known as Hamburger Head, jumped on the robber, Joe Barona from Wyoming, who was dressed as a woman. The dog knocked a water pistol out of his pocket.

Herbie Jones, of 105 Washington Avenue, threw up his baseball bank of pennies and hid behind a potted plant. When the robber attempted to escape, he slipped on the pennies, and police were able to apprehend him in time.

Mr. Paul LoPreato, bank president, said he will be expressing personal thanks to Herbie and his family today.

Mr. Jones looked up at his son and then down at the dog. "Well, you're both a couple of heroes. You saved the bank fifty thousand dollars! That's something. Come here, son." And he hugged Herbie.

Annabelle folded the paper neatly and handed it

back to Mr. Jones. "You should get some more copies. That's a nice story, Herbie." And then she headed for the door with Margie. "We'll meet at the Laurel Woods Animal Hospital in an hour. It's just two blocks from my house."

As Herbie walked outside with the girls, he called to Ray, "Come on, we have to take down the card table and TV trays. You too, Hamburger Head, let's go."

Mr. Jones put his hand on the dog. "Leave him here for a few minutes. I'll get him something to eat. I don't get a chance to feed a hero too often."

Herbie looked at Ray and raised his eyebrows. "Sure, Dad."

About ten minutes later, the boys walked around to the kitchen. They were hungry too. When they got to the screen door, Herbie ducked. "Shhh! I want to watch this," he whispered to Ray.

Mr. Jones was sitting at the table eating a bowl of SpaghettiOs. Hamburger Head was eating some off a plate next to his feet.

"Don't mind if I split a can with you," Mr. Jones said as he spooned some Os into his mouth. "Mrs. Jones will never know, either. I'll just tell her I opened a can for you. Can you keep a secret?"

Hamburger Head licked his chops and wagged his tail.

"Promise?" Mr. Jones said.

"Ruf! Ruf!" Hamburger Head barked.

"Good."

Herbie jabbed Ray and they tiptoed back to the front of the house. "We can get something to eat later. Let's leave them alone for a while. They seem to be getting along."

Herbie lay down on the front lawn and wrote a poem while Ray colored in the Burger Paradise coloring books. No one had wanted to buy them.

When Ray finished coloring, he looked up at the screen door. "Hey, your dad is watching the Yankees now."

The boys tiptoed up the stairs, lay down on their bellies, and looked in through the screen door.

The Yankees had just gotten a home run. Mr. Jones jumped off his chair and cheered. Hamburger barked and barked.

When the next batter struck out, Mr. Jones said, "Boo! That was a ball, not a strike!"

Hamburger Head walked up to the TV set and growled.

Herbie and Ray looked at each other. They were hopeful.

9

The Unlucky Cigar

At three o'clock, Herbie, Ray, and Hamburger Head met the girls at the Laurel Woods Animal Hospital.

Annabelle was waiting for them in the lobby with her ALH handbag. It contained the profits of the wag sale—$40.60.

Margie was standing by the sign that said "Laurel Woods Animal Hospital: Le-en Nguyen, DVM." "What does 'DVM' stand for next to the doctor's name?"

"Probably the D has something to do with dogs," Ray said, feeling smart.

Annabelle didn't say anything. She wasn't sure what the letters stood for.

"Well," Ray said as they walked up the porch, "I was thinking maybe we could all get a bite to eat afterward with our extra moola."

"Raymond Martin," Annabelle replied. "All of our wag sale money goes for Hamburger Head. That's why Margie and I came along today. We wanted to be sure the fund was used properly."

"Maybe Hamburger Head would like a hamburger," Ray suggested.

Annabelle pointed to her mouth. "Watch the lips, Raymond. *No* Burger Paradise."

Ray walked into the vet's office and sank down into a leather chair. He was unhappy.

Margie sat next to him and a lady holding a poodle. The poodle's paw was bandaged.

Annabelle started a conversation with someone holding a Siamese cat.

Herbie and Hamburger Head studied a giant chart of an enlarged flea.

"Hamburger Head?" a voice called.

Herbie and Annabelle walked into Dr. Nguyen's examining room.

After ten minutes, Dr. Nguyen said, "You have a mixed-breed dog that is about one and a half years old. He's half golden retriever and half beagle. He had a bad case of fleas. Best thing was to get him away from his old environment."

Herbie pictured the old beat-up car in his mind and shivered.

"I gave him a shot and a flea bath. He'll be just fine."

After the group paid the vet, bought some supplies at Price Busters and the pet shop, Annabelle said, "Well, good luck, Herbie. I hope you find a home for him."

Herbie secretly hoped that "home" was at his house. "Thanks, Annabelle and Margie, for your help."

The girls waved good-bye.

Ray didn't. He was still mad that there was no treat at Burger Paradise.

"Come on over to my house, Ray. I'll fix you a snack," said Herbie.

Ray nodded.

As the boys walked into the house, they found Mr. Jones still in the living room. He was still watching the Yankee game on television.

"Hi, boys! What did you find out?"

"The vet says he's gonna be fine."

"Where's the dog now?" Mr. Jones asked.

"On the welcome mat on the back porch."

"Well, bring him in, son. The game's not over yet. Hamburger Head can watch the ninth inning with me."

Herbie ran to get the dog.

He set him down next to his dad's green chair. "Me and Ray are getting a bite to eat now."

As the boys walked into the kitchen, Ray whispered, "Boy, Herbie, it looks like you're gettin' to first base with your dad!"

Herbie crossed both fingers.

Twenty minutes later, the boys walked back into the living room.

It was *very* quiet.

"Look," Ray whispered. "Your dad fell asleep in his chair."

Herbie looked down. Hamburger Head was sleeping next to his dad's feet.

Herbie gave Ray the A-okay sign. Then he stopped.

"Do you smell something?" he whispered.

Ray took a big whiff.

Herbie looked at Ray. "Did you pass gas?"

"No . . . did you?"

Herbie shook his head.

The boys quickly looked around the room. And then over by the door.

"Is that a cigar on the rug?" Ray whispered.

Herbie walked over to it. "That's no cigar, that's . . ."

". . . what I thought it was." Ray frowned.

Just then Mr. Jones woke up. "Hi, boys. Must have dozed off after the Yankees won. What an exciting game."

Herbie's eyes bulged. He hoped his dad wouldn't see what they just saw.

"How 'bout some coffee, Dad," Herbie suggested.

"Don't mind if I do," he said, and then as he headed for the kitchen he stopped. "Funny smell in the living room."

Mr. Jones turned around and walked back.

"Probably my cologne." Ray grinned. "It's called 'Home on the Range.' All the cowboys are wearing it now."

Herbie jabbed Ray. He was overdoing it.

"Well," Mr. Jones grumbled. "I think a better name for it would be 'Essence of Barnyard.'"

Mr. Jones went walking around. When he backed up by the door, he stepped in it!

With his bare foot!

Herbie covered his eyes with his hands.

Ray hid behind the green chair.

Hamburger Head woke up and stretched.

"GET THAT DOG OUT OF HERE!" Mr. Jones bellowed.

Hamburger Head ran behind the green chair and shivered next to Ray.

Herbie picked up the dog and put him outside. "Dad, look at where the dog doo is. He tried to get out, but you were asleep. He was trapped. It was an *accident*."

"I know where that doo is. ON MY FOOT!"

Herbie dashed to the kitchen to get a bucket of soapy water and a roll of paper towels. When Herbie returned, his dad was still seething.

"Want to put your foot in this bucket, Dad?"

"Not really. What I would like to put in the bucket is THAT DOG!"

Just then the phone rang. Olivia came in from

81

the bathroom to answer it. She had a towel wrapped around her and her hair was in curlers. "You two are supposed to be getting ready. We're going out to dinner tonight, remember?"

Herbie suddenly remembered. He had forgotten to tell Ray!

"It's for you, Dad," Olivia said. "It's Mr. LoPreato."

Mr. Jones dragged the bucket of soapy water across the living-room floor. When he finally reached the phone, Herbie ducked down next to the green chair, where Ray was still hiding. He had to talk to him.

"I'm fine," Mr. Jones said with a half-smile. "How are you, Mr. LoPreato?"

Herbie looked at Ray and rolled his eyeballs.

"Five-thirty a limousine will arrive at our house?"

Olivia ran back to the bathroom.

"Dinner at Chef Fiorelli's? Yes. We love Italian food. Yes, I think Herbie and Ray do too. Thank you, Mr. LoPreato."

As soon as Mr. Jones hung up, Herbie whispered, "Did you hear that, Ray? We're going to

dinner. Run home and get ready. And it's dressy, so wear a coat and tie."

"WE'LL GO ONE MORE NIGHT WITH THAT DOG, AND THEN TOMORROW HE GOES TO THE POUND!" Mr. Jones yelled as he dragged the bucket and banged on the bathroom door.

"No foolin'? We get free eats tonight?" Ray asked.

"Yeah, Italian food."

"Great. I even know a little Italian. I've been watching Chef Roberto Romano on TV."

"Fine, Ray. Just be ready by five-thirty."

Ray ran out of the house calling, "A RIVER DARE CHEE!"

Herbie had no idea what Ray was trying to say. He just hoped that tonight might be special enough to make up for what had happened this afternoon.

10

The Limousine

Olivia opened the bathroom door. "Who put this awful-looking daisy poster in here?"

Mr. Jones dragged the bucket inside. "Can I use the bathroom now?"

Olivia ran into the living room and looked at the clock. It was five-fifteen. "I can't believe a limousine is coming to *my* house."

"Did anyone see my black heels?" Mrs. Jones called from the bedroom.

"IN THE BATHROOM UNDER THE HAMPER," Olivia shouted.

Mr. Jones stepped out into the hall. "Who put

that horrible-looking daisy poster over the toilet?"

Herbie ran into his dad's room. "Do you have a tie I can borrow? Mine has catsup on it."

Mr. Jones walked into his closet. Herbie noticed he was wearing striped boxer shorts. They were the color of the flag.

"Well, I have two clean ones left. One you gave me for Christmas I didn't even take out of the box, and this red one."

"I'll take the red one."

When Mr. Jones looked at the tie in the box, he said, "Oh my goodness, I forgot. There's a dog on this one."

"HERBIE, DID YOU BRUSH YOUR TEETH?" Mrs. Jones called.

"Yes, Mom."

"HENRY, DID YOU BRUSH YOUR TEETH?" she repeated.

Mr. Jones made a face, then stomped out of the bedroom.

Mrs. Jones bumped into him. "Did you put that daisy poster in the bathroom?"

Olivia walked up to her brother. "Herbie, do I look okay?"

Herbie looked at his sister while he buttoned up his suit jacket. Her hair was soft and curly. He liked the way it sat on her shoulders. He liked the pink ribbon and her long pink dress. Herbie thought she looked like a movie star. She was beautiful.

"Well, how do I look?" Olivia asked.

"Okay," Herbie said.

Olivia groaned, but stopped when she heard a knock at the door. She raced back to her mother. "Are you ready?"

"Do I have lipstick on my teeth?" Mrs. Jones asked.

"No, Mom, but what's the green stuff?"

"WHAT?"

"I'm just kidding, Mom."

"That's *not* funny."

"SOMEONE'S KNOCKING AT THE DOOR!" Mr. Jones bellowed from the bedroom.

Herbie stepped up and answered it.

A man in a tuxedo and leather cap stood at the door. "Good evening," he said. "I am your driver. Your car is waiting for you."

Herbie stepped back on Olivia's foot.

She managed to smile in her pain.

"We'll be there in a moment," she said.

"Mr. LoPreato has a gift for the dog on the front lawn."

Mr. Jones stood behind his children. "How kind. We'll be right out."

Mr. Jones turned to his wife. "I'm a guy who walks to work. Now here's somebody who wants to drive me to dinner?"

Mrs. Jones smiled.

The Jones family stepped outside. Hamburger Head followed them down the steps.

"Wow!" Herbie said. "Look at that doghouse on the lawn. It's huge."

When Herbie got closer, he discovered a gold plaque. "Gee, Dad. Look at this!"

Mr. Jones leaned over and read aloud: "'From Laurel Woods State Bank, for meritorious service to the community. Hamburger Head is hereby recognized and acclaimed as First Dog of the City.' Wow!" Mr. Jones said.

Hamburger Head walked over and poked his head inside. He pawed at the red rug.

Mr. Jones shook his head. "This dog is getting

wall-to-wall carpeting before we do."

When the Jones family started to get into the limousine, Mr. LoPreato got out. He was a tall man with white hair and a white mustache. "It's an honor to meet you, Herbie. Thank you for saving us thousands of dollars."

Herbie shook Mr. LoPreato's hand.

"I'd like to meet your dog now."

Mr. Jones raised his eyebrows when he said "your dog."

"Hamburger Head," Herbie called into the doghouse. "Someone would like to meet you."

The dog came out and wagged his tail.

"Well! You did get wounded in battle, didn't you!"

"He had a flea problem, sir. But I took him to the vet, and she said he would be okay. He had a shot and a bath. A flea bath."

Mr. LoPreato smiled. Then he leaned over and shook the dog's paw. "You are a hero, Hamburger Head. The bank thanks you."

Then Herbie watched the bank president pull something out of a white foil bag. Here's a filet mignon for you."

Mr. LoPreato and Herbie watched Hamburger Head chomp and smack at the rare piece of cooked meat.

When they got back inside the limo, Mr. LoPreato handed Herbie a certificate. "On behalf of the Laurel Woods State Bank, I am giving you a five-hundred-dollar bond as a token of our appreciation."

"Thank you, sir," Herbie said.

Mr. and Mrs. Jones beamed.

As the limousine swung around the block to pick up Raymond, Mr. LoPreato said, "Like your tie, Mr. Jones."

"It's one of my favorites!" said Herbie's dad.

Herbie looked at his dad. Was it possible that he *might* have a change of heart about the dog?

11

Chef Fiorelli's

As the limousine parked in front of Raymond's house, Olivia leaned over and whispered to her brother, "I hope Raymond doesn't embarrass me."

"No problem," Herbie said.

He watched the chauffeur walk through the knee-high grass to the front porch. When he got to the steps, Shadow came from around the side and growled at him in a low tone.

Herbie knew what that meant.

Shadow thought the chauffeur was a robber or murderer.

Everyone watched as Ray came out the door.

He had his dad's white shirt on, his dad's black tie, and his dad's black coat. The coat dragged down the porch steps as he followed the chauffeur to the car.

Olivia sank down in the leather seat. "Could I possibly be *more* embarrassed?"

As soon as the door opened, Ray said, "Bone Journey."

"I could," grumbled Olivia.

"*Buon giorno!*" Mr. LoPreato replied. "I didn't realize you spoke Italian, Raymond."

"Call me Raymondo Martino," he said as he put his hand out.

Mr. LoPreato went to shake Ray's hand, but he couldn't find it. The coat sleeve was too long.

Mr. and Mrs. Jones smiled.

Herbie rolled his eyeballs. Ray was being a big shot.

"Well, Raymondo, I'm Mr. LoPreato, president of the Laurel Woods State Bank. I'm glad you could join us tonight."

Then he handed Ray a savings bond for a hundred dollars. "The bank would like to apologize for the inconvenience of that robbery. We're so thankful you stayed behind the potted plant."

Ray pulled up his sleeve. "You're giving me a hundred bucks for hiding behind a plant?"

Mr. LoPreato smiled. "Well, Raymondo, we appreciate your good thinking. When you're eighteen, you'll get money from this savings bond."

"Wow! Thanks!" Ray replied, looking at the certificate. "I've heard of James Bond, but not Savings Bond. Do you think they're related?"

Olivia pressed the window button. She needed fresh air.

When she got a hot blast of wind in her face, she quickly pressed the button again.

She forgot the limousine was air-conditioned.

Herbie jabbed his buddy. "I think you should cool it, Raymondo."

As the limousine drove out of town and along the Connecticut River, the grown-ups talked. The boys looked out the back window while Olivia pretended she was Cinderella going to the ball.

When the limousine finally arrived at Chef Fiorelli's, two men dressed in uniforms and caps opened the car door.

Both of them knew Mr. LoPreato.

Ray whispered to Herbie. "This LoPreato guy is the biggest big shot I've ever met."

As they walked inside the lobby and checked their coats, Herbie looked around. He had never been to a fancy restaurant like this before.

When he looked out at the big room where people were eating, he saw the huge gold chandeliers and the big fireplace.

Ray noticed the marble statue next to the fireplace. "That dude is nude!"

Herbie looked. "Yeah. Good thing that guy is next to the fire. He won't catch cold."

The boys cracked up.

Olivia noticed the lady in front of them. She was wearing a white mink stole and her hair was piled high on her head.

She whispered to Herbie, "Look at her hairdo!"

Herbie made a face. "It looks like she has a cinnamon roll on her head."

"Herbie, *that* is called a chignon. It's very fashionable."

The waiter seated the LoPreato party next to the lady in the mink stole.

As everyone sat down at the large round table with the white linen tablecloth, white linen napkins stuffed in crystal glasses, white candles, and one long-stem rose in a cut-glass vase, Herbie said, "You can sure tell this is a fancy place. Look at all the breadsticks on the table!"

Olivia kicked her brother. "Fancy things are wasted on you," she whispered. Then she leaned forward and sniffed the red rose.

Herbie reached for two breadsticks. "En garde, Signor Raymondo," he said, tossing Ray one.

Ray caught it with his right hand. As he put his left hand behind his back, the boys began their sword fight.

Tsk! Tsk! Tsk! went the breadsticks.

By the time Mr. Jones realized what they were doing, it was too late. Both breadsticks broke in two and one of the pieces went flying in the air like a missile.

Olivia dropped her mouth. Mr. Jones started to sweat. Mrs. Jones shot Herbie a look.

Mr. LoPreato raised his eyebrows as he watched the flight of the breadstick.

When it started to descend on the lady in the mink stole, Herbie watched it carefully.

Plunk!

It landed right on her hairdo.

Right in the middle of her cinnamon roll. Bull's-eye! Herbie thought.

Mr. LoPreato patted Herbie's arm. "Actually, that breadstick adds something. I'd call it high fashion."

Herbie was surprised everyone at the table was watching, especially Mr. LoPreato. Herbie straightened his tie and tried to smile.

Mr. Jones wiped his brow with his linen napkin. He was glad Mr. LoPreato had a sense of humor.

"Well," the bank president said as he fiddled with his mustache. "What would you like to order?"

Everyone studied their large red menu.

"I can't find cheeseburgers on here," Ray said.

Herbie whispered, "This is an Italian restaurant, *Raymondo*."

"Yeah, you're right," Ray said, and he went back to read his menu some more.

"The veal saltimbocca is delicious!" Mr. Lo-Preato suggested. "I always have it when I come here. Chef Fiorelli does it just right."

Olivia put her menu down. "I would like to try the veal, thank you," she said.

"I'll have the eggplant parmigiana," Mrs. Jones said. "I'm trying to keep to a fruit-and-vegetable diet. Right, Henry?"

Mr. Jones grumbled.

"Well, what will it be, boys?" Mr. LoPreato asked.

Ray put his menu down. "I don't get it. This is *supposed* to be an Italian restaurant, and there's no pizza, no meatballs, and no SpaghettiOs on the menu."

Olivia cringed.

Mr. LoPreato snapped his fingers. A waiter came and left. When he returned, Mr. LoPreato said, "Chef Fiorelli would be happy to fix you a special plate of spaghetti and meatballs, Raymondo."

"Brave O," Ray replied.

"Bravo!" Mr. LoPreato agreed.

"I think I'll have that too!" Herbie said.

"Me too."

Everyone looked at Mr. Jones. "I love spaghetti, even though I don't get it around the house," he said, glaring at his wife.

"Make that three orders," Mr. LoPreato said to the waiter.

Then he looked at Raymond. "So, you have a dog too?"

"Yes, his name is Shadow. He's kind of lazy, but he can spot a robber or murderer real easy. He protects our house good," Ray replied.

Mr. LoPreato smiled as he curled his mustache. "Kind of like Herbie's dog. He protected our bank from the robber and saved us lots of money."

Herbie was glad the waiter brought their food. He didn't know what to say.

And he didn't say anything else the rest of the meal.

When his dad asked for a doggy bag for his spaghetti and meatballs, Herbie wondered, Was his dad trying to make his dog's last meal a good one?

12

The Decision

That night when the Joneses got home, Herbie ran right to the doghouse.

"HE'S NOT HERE!" he called out.

Olivia twirled her pink dress in the kitchen. "I felt like Cinderella tonight! Someday . . . I'm going to marry a man like Mr. LoPreato, and we'll have veal saltimbocca every night for dinner."

Then she stopped twirling.

"It would have been a perfect evening if Raymond Martin hadn't come along."

Herbie ran to the welcome mat on the back porch. Hamburger Head wasn't there.

"That spaghetti was out of this world," Mr. Jones said as he leaned back in his big green chair. "And to think Chef Fiorelli made it special just for me."

Mrs. Jones sighed. "Maybe I'll make you some spaghetti next week, dear. You really do love it, don't you?"

Mr. Jones kissed his fingers. "Bravo!"

"Wasn't Mr. LoPreato generous!" Olivia exclaimed.

"Yes," Mrs. Jones agreed. "Imagine a savings bond for our Herbie and . . . Raymondo."

Olivia made a face.

Herbie ran outside to the backyard. He looked at the blue blanket under his bedroom window.

No Hamburger Head.

Herbie waited in the backyard for a full five minutes; then he turned, put his head down, and walked back into the house.

"It was an evening our family will remember for a long time," Mrs. Jones said. "I just wish we had brought our camera."

Herbie plopped on the couch. "Doesn't *anybody* care? My dog is gone!"

"*Your* dog?" Mr. Jones replied.

Herbie shouted, "YES, *MY* DOG!" Then he lowered his voice. "For one more night."

As he looked over at his dad, his eyes bulged.

There was Hamburger Head sitting at his dad's feet, licking his lips. An empty foil tray of spaghetti was next to him.

Herbie got up slowly. "You . . . you let him in, Dad? And you . . . you fed him?"

Mr. Jones stroked the dog's golden fur. He didn't say anything.

Herbie stood next to his dad now. "Is that his last supper?"

Herbie didn't move. He was waiting for his dad's words.

"Well, it's kind of tough to kick the First Dog of the City out of our house."

Herbie dived on his dad's lap and threw his arms around him. "Oh, Dad, do you *really* mean it?"

"I *really* mean it, son. You can have a dog as long as it's this one. He's a Yankee fan who loves spaghetti. That makes him special."

"Like you, Dad."

And then they hugged like bears.

13

The Pet Party

Sunday afternoon after church, Herbie invited
Ray and Shadow, Annabelle and Sukey, and Margie and Tiger to his backyard for a party.

He made paper hats for all the pets.

Shadow's hat was a Viking helmet.

Sukey's had fish all over it.

Tiger's hat had stripes.

And Hamburger Head's hat had hamburgers
on it.

"I think such a happy occasion calls for song!"
Annabelle exclaimed, and she took out her harmonica from her ALH handbag and hummed the
first note.

"Hamburger Head, this is for you."
Everyone listened on the lawn next to his pet.

"How much is that doggie in the window?
Ruf! Ruf!
The one with the waggily tail . . .
How much is that doggie in the window?
Ruf! Ruf!
I do hope that doggie's for sale."

Herbie thought Annabelle's noodle curls kept good time to the beat.

"I've got a song too," Herbie said. "Everyone knows it, so you can sing along. It's 'Bingo'!"

Ray clapped. "I even know the words to *that*."

Shadow barked.

Hamburger Head barked.

Sukey and Tiger meowed.

"The pets do too," Herbie called out. "Everyone sing:

'There was a farmer had a dog
And Bingo was his name-o
B–I–N–G–O
B–I–N–G–O
B–I–N–G–O
And Bingo was his name-o.

'There was a farmer had a dog
And Bingo was his name-o
CLAP I–N–G–O
CLAP I–N–G–O
CLAP I–N–G–O
And Bingo was his name-o.

'There was a farmer had a dog
And Bingo was his name-o
CLAP, CLAP N–G–O
CLAP, CLAP N–G–O
CLAP, CLAP N–G–O
And Bingo was his name-o.'"

Just as they were all clapping and singing the last verse of "Bingo," Mr. Jones brought out a plate of day-old Dipping Donuts.

"Come and get it!" he yelled.

The dogs and Sukey and Tiger came racing over to see what Mr. Jones had on the plate.

As soon as he lowered it, the pets turned around and walked back across the lawn.

Annabelle picked a donut up and, when she felt how hard it was, put it back down. "I'm not hungry, thank you."

Margie copied Annabelle and said, "No, thank you."

Herbie and Ray took two. "You gotta be tough," Ray said as he took a big bite in a chocolate-frosted cake donut.

Herbie chomped into a powdered one. "Yeah, real tough."

"I have one more dog song," Ray said with his mouth full. And he started clicking his fingers:

"You ain't nothin' but a houndog,
    cryin' all the time.
You ain't nothin' but a houndog,
    cryin' all the time.

"You ain't never caught a rabbit,
    and you ain't no friend of
    mine."

After Ray finished singing, Annabelle picked up Sukey and Margie picked up Tiger. "See you both in school Thursday," Annabelle said.

Then the girls left.

Herbie and Ray sat at the picnic table and looked at their dogs.

They were asleep in the shade. Shadow had his paw around Hamburger Head.

"I told you they were gonna be great friends," Ray said to Herbie.

Herbie nodded. "Like us, Ray. Like us."